D06739 08

# SIR LANCE A-LITTLE

*For my son, Gregory – a real life pocket hero*
D.W.

*For Ross, Ray and Charlie – three brave men, indeed*
C.I.

ORCHARD BOOKS
338 Euston Road, London NW1 3BH
*Orchard Books Australia*
Level 17/207 Kent Street, Sydney, NSW 2000

First published in 2013
First paperback publication in 2014

ISBN 978 1 40831 354 1 (hardback)
ISBN 978 1 40831 360 2 (paperback)

Text and illustrations © Dave Woods and Chris Inns 2013

The rights of Dave Woods and Chris Inns to be identified as the authors and illustrators of this work have been asserted by them in accordance with the Copyright, Designs and Patents Act, 1988.

A CIP catalogue record for this book is available from the British Library.

1 3 5 7 9 10 8 6 4 2 (hardback)
1 3 5 7 9 10 8 6 4 2 (paperback)

Printed in Great Britain

Orchard Books is a division of Hachette Children's Books, an Hachette UK company.

www.hachette.co.uk

# SIR LANCE A-LITTLE

DAVE WOODS
CHRIS INNS

ORCHARD

Knights, as we know, have always been famous for their courage. But before knights were knights – they were squires. And there was one young squire who was as brave as brave could be (perhaps even braver).

His name was *Sir Lance-a-Little*!

A long time ago, knights roamed the land.

And when knights weren't roaming the land, they were busy telling tales about their adventures. Their favourite place to meet was on a bridge in London.

It was called *Knightsbridge*.

One fine day – legend says – a new knight came to Knightsbridge. He was a young knight, hungry for adventure, with a lance in one hand and a packed lunch in the other.

He went by the name of Sir Lance-a-Little.

"GOOD MORNING, GOOD KNIGHTS!" cried Sir Lance-a-Little. There was a rattle of armour as great knights looked up from telling even greater stories.

"Er, pardon?" said a large, barrel-chested knight. It was Sir Flagon of Ale.

"My name is Sir Lance-a-Little." Sir Lance-a-Little pulled out a list (which was longer than he was).

"I AM ON A QUEST!" cried the little knight.

"Short trip, is it?" grinned Sir Flagon.

There was a ripple of laughter.

"I HAVE NO TIME TO WASTE!" exclaimed Sir Lance-a-Little.

"Yes," agreed Sir Reginald Rustybottom. "Time is short!"

More tinny tittering.

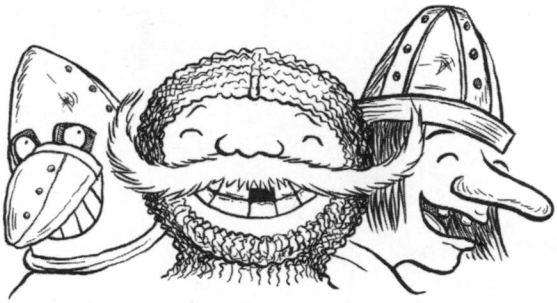

"To complete my quest," Sir Lance-a-Little continued, in a small but noble voice, "I need some brave knights to join me!"

A hush fell over the knights. Laughter ceased. For the one thing knights take seriously (more seriously even than new anti-rust products) is a chance to prove their bravery.

But before anyone could step forward, Sir Lance-a-Little's eye was drawn to one group of knights in particular…

A group that huddled together fiercely.

"Ah, brave knights!" said Sir Lance-a-Little. "I see you are united by courage!"

(Actually, it was fear.)

"And your swords shake in readiness for the quest!" he added.

(No, they were just scared.)

"What do they call thee?" asked Sir Lance-a-Little.

"They call us... *THE COWARDS OF CAMELOT!*" said Quaver the Minstrel, their travelling musician.

"Then ride with me, Cowards of Camelot!" Sir Lance-a-Little checked his Quest List. "We shall fight terrible ogres..."

The Cowards took a step backwards.

"We shall defeat evil wizards..." the little knight continued.

The Cowards took another step back.

"We shall slay fierce dragons..."

And another step back.

"We shall, er…"

Sir Lance-a-Little thought for a moment – then continued.

"We shall...eat cake!"

"CAKE?" said Sir Render, one of the Cowards, as they all stepped forward. "What sort of cake?"

"Oh, chocolate muffins. Fondant fancies. Typical banquet-type treats you get at the end of a quest," said Sir Lance-a-Little.

"And puddings, too?" asked Sir Hugo First.

"Verily," said Sir Lance-a-Little. "With custard!"

(Verily is a knight's way of saying 'yes'.)

The Cowards had a hurried huddle. Then they came forward again.

"We're in!" they whispered.

And they were. Because they may have been cowardly – but they loved their custard!

SIR LANCE-A-LITTLE
At being brave
Sir Lance is best.
The knight to lead us
On this quest!
SIR RENDER
He always carries
A big, white tissue.
So quick surrender
Is never an issue!

SIR HUGO FIRST
Sir Hugo's first
When he sees trouble.
To beat a retreat
And at the double!
LADY GWYNETH FEAR
Fear by name
And fear by nature.
This lady's for turning
Away from danger!

PERCIVAL POOP-DE-PANTS
William the Conkerer
Was a distant cousin.
And Percy gets distant
When trouble is coming!
SIR CUMFERENCE
This big, round knight
Built a big, round table.
To hide underneath it
He was able!

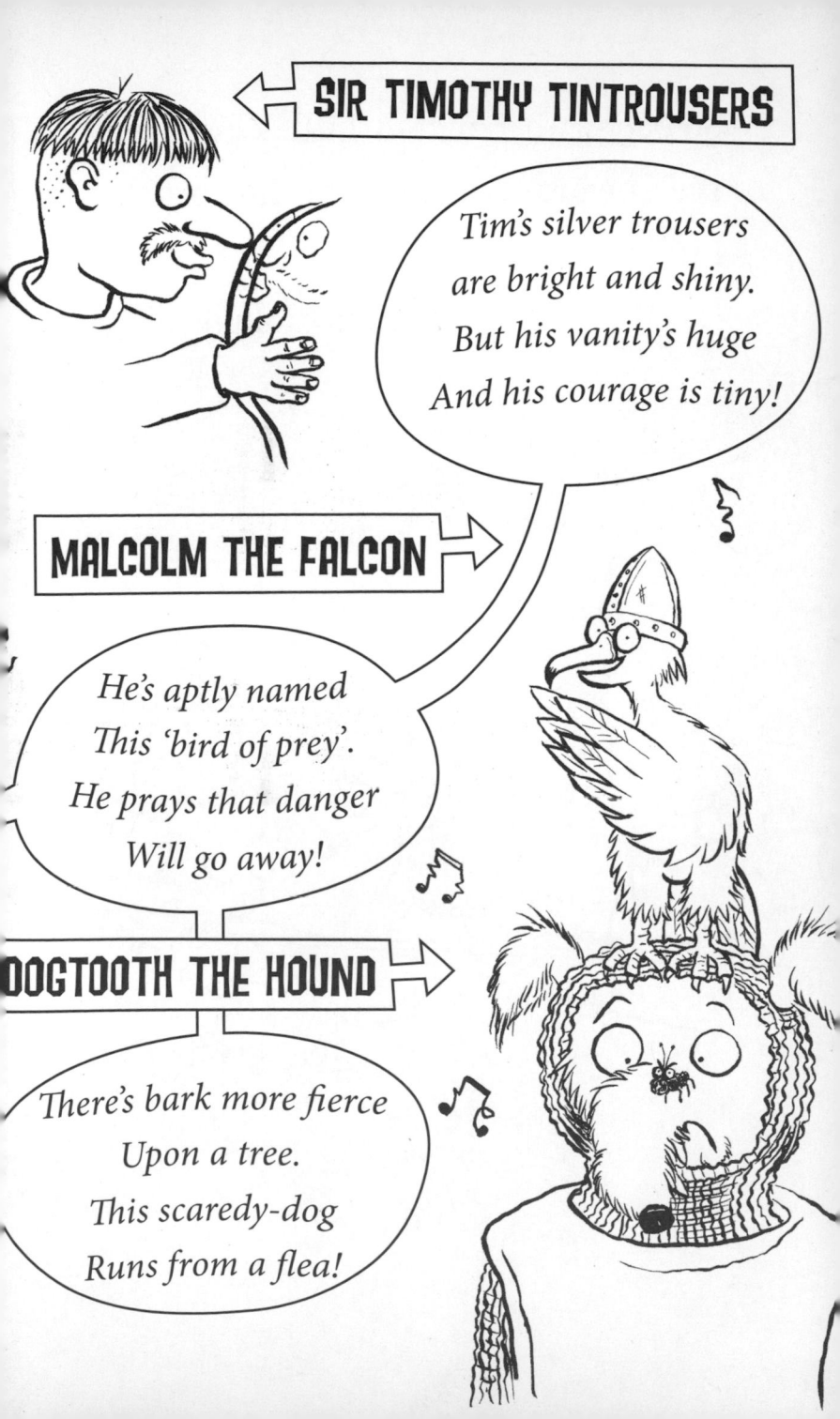
SIR TIMOTHY TINTROUSERS
Tim's silver trousers
are bright and shiny.
But his vanity's huge
And his courage is tiny!
MALCOLM THE FALCON
He's aptly named
This 'bird of prey'.
He prays that danger
Will go away!
DOGTOOTH THE HOUND
There's bark more fierce
Upon a tree.
This scaredy-dog
Runs from a flea!

So began Sir Lance-a-Little's quest, with the Cowards of Camelot riding beside him.

(Well, behind him, actually.)

Sir Lance-a-Little checked his Quest List.

"The first task is tricky," he said. "We need to defeat a wizard."

"An evil wizard?" squawked Sir Percival Poop-de-Pants.

"Verily," replied the little knight. "The sort of wizard that puts the evil in medieval."

"Oh, dear…" said Sir Render.

Sir Lance-a-Little pulled a copy of 'Which Wizard?' from his saddlebag. "We must head to the village of Magic Wandsworth. Apparently, there's an evil wizard there."

So they did.

And there was.

He was called GONDAFT THE WIZARD.

(He'd gone daft by mixing up his spellbooks with his cookbooks. And as he was a very bad cook – his magic was very bad, too.)

"GONDAFT THE WIZARD!" yelled Sir Lance-a-Little. "You have cooked up nothing but trouble – and a few dozen wing-of-bat-flavoured pastries – for the people of Camelot. Get thee gone!"

"I AM NOT GOING ANYWHERE! I SHALL COOK A SPELL UPON THEE!" raged Gondaft. (Evil wizards say that sort of thing.)

He pointed his wooden spoon at the cowardly knights. The air began to crackle with magic (and the smell of fried onions).

**"ABRA-KEBABRA!
KNIGHT, FALCON, DOG.
I'LL CHANGE YOU TO CAKES
EACH SHAPED LIKE A FROG!"**

Gondaft's spoon sizzled and a bolt of delicious-smelling magic drifted towards Sir Lance-a-Little.

But, at the last moment, the little knight pulled Sir Timothy Tintrousers in front of him. The vain knight's super-shiny armour reflected the evil wizard's cookery spell straight back at him!

Hey Pesto! Gondaft was turned into a cream-filled, frog-shaped cake.

"Well, he got his just desserts," said Sir Timothy Tintrousers.

Sir Lance-a-Little agreed, then put a cherry on top of Gondaft – and a big tick on his Quest List!

"Next," read Sir Lance-a-Little, "we must save a DAMSEL IN DISTRESS!"

So they searched high and low for a tower (well, mainly high) until they found one.

It was very white and very tall.

(But mainly, very tall.)

"SAVE ME!" cried a Damsel in Distress from the upper window.

(Damsels in Distress always say that.)

"Er, we're scared of heights!" pointed out the Cowards. (No surprise there.)

Sir Cumference held his long lance up to the tower to show just how high it was…

And suddenly, Sir Lance-a-Little was scurrying up the lance like a little metal-plated monkey!

Up he climbed.

Higher.

Higher.

Dangerously

higher.

Until – he reached the tower window!

The Cowards burst into applause. (Which made a change from them bursting into tears.)

"I'm Alice from the Palace!" squealed the delighted Damsel. Then she gave Sir Lance-a-Little a big, slobbery kiss.

Yuk! he thought. (Knights don't do kissing.)

"Come, my lady," he said. "We must away!"

"Are we going somewhere?" she asked. "I must change – I can't go out in my dressing-gown!"

"We're in a hurry, my lady," urged Sir Lance-a-Little, trying to be polite. "You see, I'm on a quest..."

"Not so fast, junior!" snapped Alice. "I've got an important decision to make."

"An important decision?"

She grabbed two outfits from her wardrobe. "Now, should I be a Damsel in Dis-dress? Or Dat-dress?"

Sir Lance-a-Little nodded politely... and backed towards the window.

Alice pulled out more dresses. "Now, let me think..."

Sir Lance-a-Little slid back down Sir Cumference's lance.

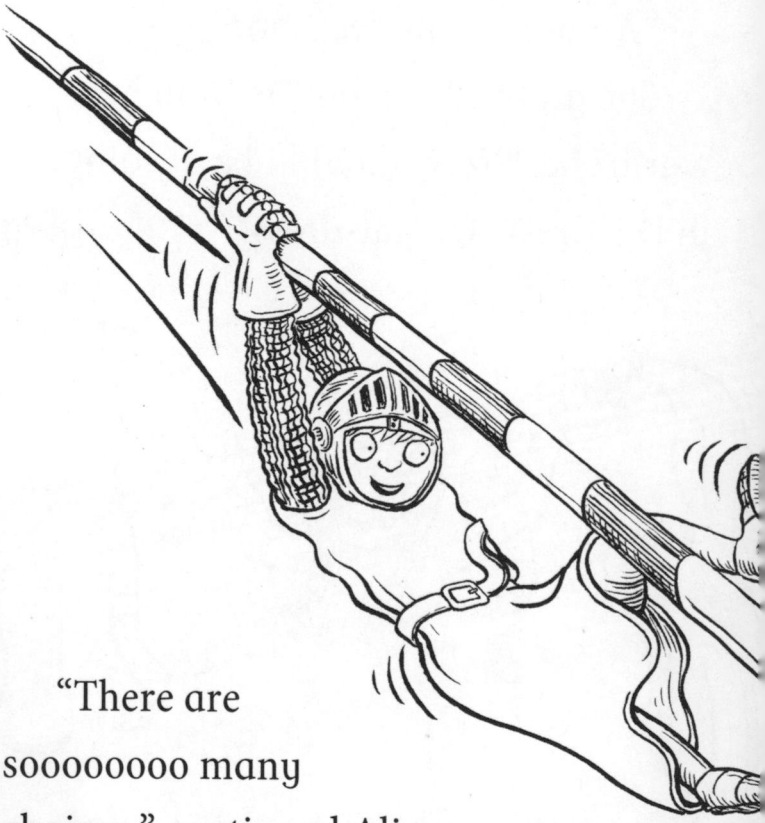

"There are soooooooo many choices," continued Alice.

And she was still chattering to herself as the cowardly knights – led by Sir Lance-a-Little – rode away.

"She seemed nice, didn't she?" said Sir Render. "But in the end she was a bit of an Ogre…"

"Funny you should mention OGRES," grinned Sir Lance-a-Little, checking his list, "because that's our next challenge!"

"Oh, dear…" said Sir Render.

Later, the band of knights approached a large stone bridge.

From underneath it came a terrible roar.

"ROOOOOOAAAAAAARRRR!"

(Told you it was terrible.)

The terrible roar was accompanied by a terrible Ogre. (Which made sense.)

"For you to pass over my bridge," growled the Ogre, "I must eat the bravest amongst you!"

(Ogres are partial to brave knights. Peeled, of course.)

Sir Lance-a-Little whispered something to Sir Hugo First. The cowardly knight then edged nervously onto the bridge…

"Oh, don't eat me, Mr Ogre," cried Sir Hugo. "There's a much braver, and therefore more delicious knight behind me…"

"Very well, pass then!" bellowed the ogre.

Next up was Lady Gwyneth Fear. "Don't eat me either, Mr Ogre. For following me is a knight so brave, he's truly scrumptious..."

"Hmm, pass then!" boomed the Ogre. (Who, to be honest, thought he'd heard this somewhere before.)

Eventually, all the Cowards used the same trick to pass the Ogre. Who, by now, had worked up a monstrous appetite. "Where's my dinner?" he howled.

"Down here!" cried Sir Lance-a-Little, waving his tiny sword. "Try and eat me if thee dare!"

"Huh?" grunted the Ogre.

He looked down at the brave – but tiny – knight.

"You're no dinner!" he roared. "You're not even a nibble!"

And with that, the disappointed Ogre stomped off downriver in a huff.

"It'll have to be Fisherman Pie for supper," he grumbled. "Or maybe Shepherd Pie…"

Sir Lance-a-Little checked his Quest List again. "We must win a JOUSTING TOURNAMENT!" he cried.

The knights rode to the town of Little Riding, where the 'Joust-a-Minute' Jousting Tournament was taking place.

"Perfect," said Sir Lance-a-Little.

Now, a knight can't joust without a valiant steed to joust upon.

(A valiant steed is fancy knight talk for a horse.)

So it was that Sir Lance-a-Little entered the tournament on his, er… Shetland Pony.

The other colourful knights in the tournament looked at his small pony.

"Art thou feeling a little horse?" the Green Knight giggled.

"As knights go, thou art surely the shortest!" the Red Knight laughed.

"We'll see who laugheth the longest," replied Sir Lance-a-Little.

A fanfare sounded. The tournament began…

"Oh, dear…" said Sir Render, as the Cowards looked on.

But, guess what?

Sir Lance-a-Little was so small – none of the other knights could spike him.

And the other knights were so big – the little knight couldn't miss them.

Lo and behold…

SIR LANCE-A-LITTLE WON!

The Green Knight was hugely envious.

The Red Knight was greatly embarrassed.

And the Black and Blue Knights were bruised all over.

"The bigger they are, the harder they falleth!" smiled Sir Lance-a-Little.

"Just one more task!" exclaimed Sir Lance-a-Little, holding his Quest List up high.

"What is it?"

"Guess..."

"Give us a clue," said the Cowards.

"It rhymes with FLAGON," replied the little knight.

"Oh, dear..." said Sir Render.

They rode (reluctantly) until they came to a mountain.

In the side of the mountain…was a great, dark cave.

And in the great, dark cave lived… (well, you can guess).

"I'm going in!" cried Sir Lance-a-Little.

"We're going home!" whimpered the Cowards of Camelot.

"BE STILL, BRAVE KNIGHTS!" ordered the little knight.

So the Cowards of Camelot stood at the great, dark cave entrance and waited…

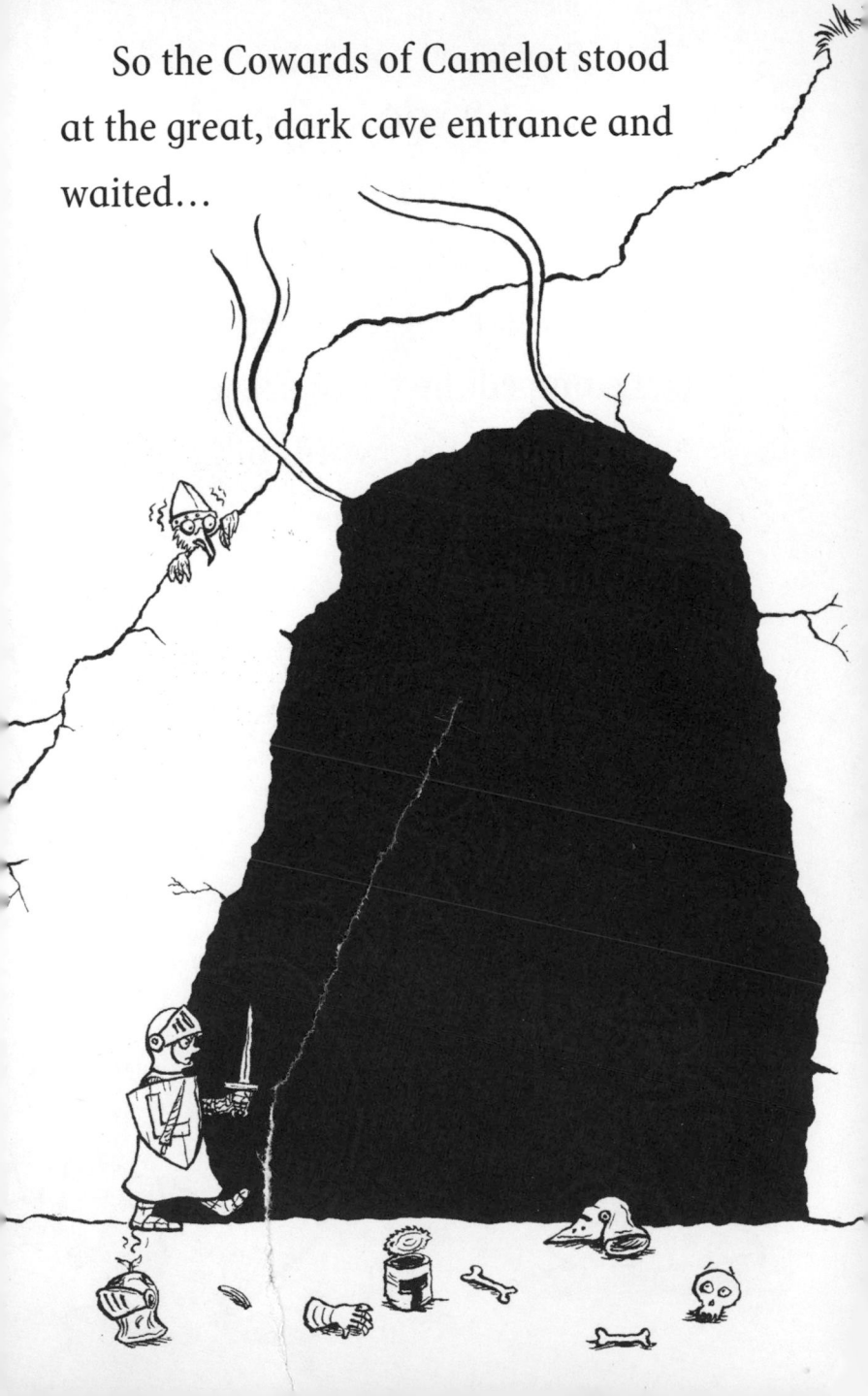

"COME OUT, THOU FIRE-BREATHING DRAGON!" yelled Sir Lance-a-Little. "THESE KNIGHTS BE NOT AFRAID!" (Which, as we know, wasn't strictly true.)

Out stomped the fierce dragon.

Amazingly, the Cowards of Camelot didn't run away (because they were frozen with fear).

"I'LL SKEWER YOU KNIGHTS AND BARBECUE MYSELF A CAMELOT KEBAB!" roared the dragon.

The knights quivered like jellies.

"OR MAYBE I'LL ROAST YOU SIRS LIKE SIR-LOIN STEAKS!"

The knights' knees knocked together.

But – while the dragon was unleashing its (fiery) temper – Sir Lance-a-Little sneaked around the back of the cave. And as the dragon was about to breathe a scorching blast of fire…the tiny knight pulled out his little lance and jabbed the dragon – in the bum!

"WHAT?!!!!?"

The dragon was so surprised… instead of breathing fire out – it sucked fire in!

"ERIF!"
And burnt itself to a cinder!
The Cowards were certain
Their ending had come.
But Lance spiked that dragon
Right in his big...
ENOUGH!

"MY QUEST FOR BRAVERY IS OVER!" cried Sir Lance-a-Little, making one final tick before rolling up his list. "Now, I must hurry back to my master."

"Your master?" asked the Cowards. "Who is your master?"

"THE BLACK PRINCIPAL!" replied Sir Lance-a-Little.

The Cowards went all a-quiver. For the Black Principal had a dark reputation…for handing out terrible punishments. But if they wanted their rewards, the Cowards had to accompany Sir Lance-a-Little back to a tall, dark castle.

There, Sir Lance-a-Little knocked on a tall, dark door – which was answered by a tall, dark stranger.

It was THE BLACK PRINCIPAL!

But the Cowards of Camelot noticed something…

"Sir Lance-a-Little is scared, too!" they whispered.

And he was. His little teeth were a-chattering.

The Black Principal looked down at the tiny knight. "Have you completed your quest, Sir Lance-a-Little?"

There was a pause. (A short one.)

"Yes, Sir," replied Sir Lance-a-Little. "I've finished my bravery homework."

He handed over his Quest List.

"Then you shan't be terribly punished!" said the Black Principal.

"HOMEWORK!" cried the Cowards of Camelot. "You mean he's still at school?"

"Yes," said The Black Principal. "KNIGHT SCHOOL!"

To reward Sir Lance-a-Little for completing his bravery project, the Black Principal gave him a gold star.

And to thank the Cowards of Camelot for helping, the Black Principal gave them (can you guess?) – cake!

LL KNIGHT DINER
Our brave quest is ended
The homework is done.
It's time to start feasting –
Tarts, muffins and buns!

And what became of Sir Lance-a-Little?
Well, that's another story...

FURTHER READING!
THE SMALL DRAGON VOL I by I. Seeit
THE LARGE DRAGON VOL II by I. Leggit
SAVE ME!!! by Isa Cummin
ETIQUETTE FOR KNIGHTS by Neil Downe
THE CROSSBOW by ANNE ARCHER
SUCCESSFUL QUESTS by Percy Vere
EVIL WIZARDS by Caster Badspell
DON'T LOOK UNDER BRIDGES by C. A. Troll

# JOIN THE POCKET HEROES

## FOR SOME REALLY BIG ADVENTURES!

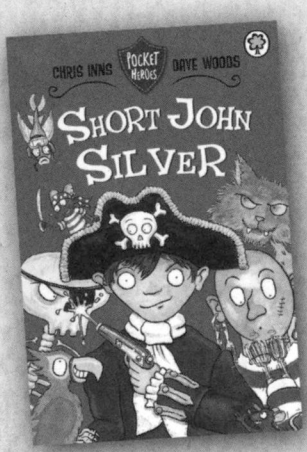


Join LOW-stature pirate Short John Silver in a HIGH-seas quest!

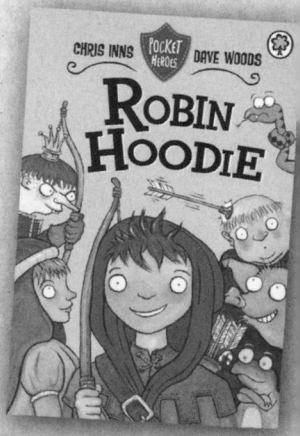


Head to Sherbet Forest with Robin Hoodie and his Merry Boyz!

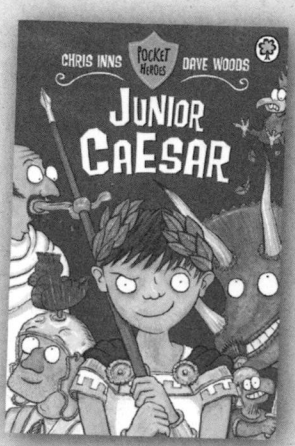


Fight the power in ancient Rome with Junior Caesar!

Clean up fairy-tale land with Florence Nightingirl and her National Elf Service!

Bring football home with pint-sized-prince, Henry 1/8th!

# COLLECT THEM ALL!

# Fairy Tale Twists

Written by Katie Dale
Illustrated by Matt Buckingham

| | |
|---|---|
| The Big Bad Werewolf | 978 1 40831 210 0 |
| Goldilocks and the Pea | 978 1 40831 211 7 |
| The Not-So-Evil Stepmother | 978 1 40831 212 4 |
| The Wickedest Witch | 978 1 40831 213 1 |
| Prince Charming's Princess Quest | 978 1 40831 214 8 |
| The Unfair-y Godmother | 978 1 40831 215 5 |
| Jack to the Rescue! | 978 1 40831 216 2 |
| Three Magic Mice | 978 1 40831 217 9 |

All priced at £8.99

Orchard Books are available from all good bookshops, or can be ordered from our website, www.orchardbooks.co.uk, or telephone 01235 827702, or fax 01235 827703.

# Max and Molly's Guide To Trouble!

## Meet Max and Molly: terrorising the neighbourhood really extremely politely...

Max and Molly's guides guarantee brilliantly funny mayhem and mischief as we learn how to be a genius, catch a criminal, build an abominable snowman and stop a Viking invasion!

978 1 40830 519 5 £4.99 Pbk
978 1 40831 572 9 eBook

978 1 40830 520 1 £4.99 Pbk
978 1 40831 573 6 eBook

978 1 40830 521 8 £4.99 Pbk
978 1 408 31574 3 eBook

978 1 40830 522 5 £4.99 Pbk
978 1 408 31575 0 eBook

ORCHARD BOOKS
www.orchardbooks.co.uk

# DAVE WOODS
# CHRIS INNS

| | |
|---|---|
| SHORT JOHN SILVER | 978 1 40831 353 4 |
| SIR LANCE-A-LITTLE | 978 1 40831 354 1 |
| ROBIN HOODIE | 978 1 40831 358 9 |
| JUNIOR CAESAR | 978 1 40831 356 5 |
| FLORENCE NIGHTINGIRL | 978 1 40831 357 2 |
| HENRY THE 1/8TH | 978 1 40831 355 8 |

All hardbacks priced at £8.99

Orchard Books are available from all good bookshops,
or can be ordered from our website: www.orchardbooks.co.uk,
or telephone 01235 827702, or fax 01235 827703.